Gingerbread Bride

Jude Knight

I0571181

Published by Jude Knight at CreateSpace
Copyright 2016 Judith Anne Knighton writing as Jude Knight

ISBN 978-0-473-35791-7

Cover image: designed by Mari Christie, gingerbread iced by Beth Fuge

Dedication

To the Bluestocking Belles, the finest group of historical romance authors on the planet. Together, we sold 15,000 copies of the box set this story first appeared in, and raised over $5,000 for the Malala Fund.

Lieutenant Rick Redepenning has been saving his admiral's intrepid daughter from danger since their formative years, but today, he faces the gravest of threats--the damage she might do to his heart. How can he convince her to see him as a suitor, not just a childhood friend?

Travelling with her father's fleet has left Mary Pritchard ill-prepared for London Society, and prey to the machinations of false friends. When she strikes out on her own to find a more suitable locale to take up her solitary spinsterhood, she finds adventure, trouble, and her girlhood hero, riding once more to her rescue.

Table of Contents

Chapter One

"I don't run away. I run towards," she had told Rick the first time he retrieved her for her father, the admiral. That was half his lifetime ago, when she was nine, and he was a young midshipman of nearly fourteen.

He sat on his horse for a moment, watching her trudging down the meadow towards the village in the valley. The Mary of today was slowed by a bandbox in one hand and a carpetbag in the other. The earnest child of his memory—chasing after a dream through a sunlit field in Spain, or Italy, or Jamaica—had never bothered with such practicalities as luggage.

Rick hadn't seen her since she was sent home to relatives after her father's death, but he couldn't mistake her. What was Miss Mary Pritchard running towards today?

The immediate destination, he could guess well enough. He'd seen the broken-down coach back around several curves of this long, winding road, and not long ago, he'd passed the coachman with a string of passengers grumbling along behind him. And pretty rough sorts some of them looked, too.

Miss Independent Mary had undoubtedly struck out on her own across country instead of sticking to the road, and would be at the inn in the valley a good half hour before the rest of the coachload.

But what was the admiral's daughter doing on a coach in the first place? The aunt she lived with was in London. Indeed, he had dropped his card at the house. He had called three times before the aunt had consented to see him, only to explain that the niece of the Dowager Viscountess Bosville could expect better than a half-pay navy lieutenant with a bad limp and few expectations. He wanted to renew his friendship, not court her, but no doubt, the aunt knew Mary's mind better than he did.

Perhaps not, though. The aunt was, indeed, in London, but Miss Mary was definitely there below him, striding across the field.

He nudged the post horse into a walk. There must be a gate along the road somewhere. Yes. There. By the time he'd dismounted, led the horse through, shut the gate, and awkwardly mounted again, Mary had reached the lowest corner of the field and was opening a gate there.

What was that movement? Three men were creeping along her side of the field, careful to stay in the shadow of the hedge. Sneak up on Mary Pritchard, would they? He'd see about that.

He kneed the horse into a gallop. The men stopped at the noise, then spun round and hurried away uphill. Mary turned to face the horse.

She stood rigid, one hand creeping into her coat. So Miss Mary was armed? That didn't surprise him. He'd taught her to shoot himself, after the incident in the date grove just outside Tunis. He still got the collywobbles thinking about the danger she'd put herself in, running off to buy a present for her father's birthday.

The slavers were congratulating themselves when he caught up with them. They had left the sweet little red-haired girl bound and helpless, and were brewing coffee and boasting of the money she would fetch. Except she'd used the flip knife he'd given her, after the escapade in the Spanish church, to cut her bonds. When he arrived, Mary, bless the courage of her, had armed herself with the rifles they'd carelessly left slung on their camels.

When he attacked, they found themselves shot at from two directions, including from their own ramshackle weapons. They might have withstood his assault, but the sight of a child with an armful of guns gave them pause. Her first wild shot convinced them that she had no idea what she was doing, but was going to do it anyway.

With no way of predicting what would happen next, they decided discretion was the better part of valor. Rick teased Mary that he'd been tempted to flee with them, given her wildly inaccurate shooting. He had no idea how it happened that they stopped at the Tunisian market to buy a woolen klim for her father before he took her safely back to the ship.

He tugged his mind back into 1799. She'd recognized him. The tension remained, but she removed her hand from her coat.

"Miss Pritchard," he said, bowing as well as he could from the back of his horse.

"Lieutenant Redepenning." She did not sound at all pleased to see him.

Richard Redepenning. What on earth was he doing in a field in Surrey? As if her running away conjured him! She almost smiled. He had appeared out of nowhere to rescue her so many times when she was young.

Then she remembered—he had been in London for two months, and hadn't called on her once. Today, she was rescuing herself, thank you very much.

Good manners, however, prompted her to say, "I was sorry to hear about your wound. I trust you are recovering?"

He was dismounting, and she could see for herself that the wound left him lame. His boot hit the ground, and he lurched, catching his balance against the saddle. She almost dropped her bags and put out a hand to help him, but she could hear her father's voice saying, "Let the man keep his pride, child."

Instead, she surreptitiously eased her shoulders. The bags had not felt nearly as heavy when she strode away from the others at the coach, after a short argument with the coachman about the merits of following the road versus trusting her navigation skills.

The coachman insisted that sticking to the road was a much better idea, since who knew what barriers might appear on the path that cut down the hill. "I know what I'm doing, Miss," he insisted. If he thought she was going to trust a coachman who had finally landed them in the ditch after multiple near misses, he was soon disabused of the notion.

As soon as she struck out on her own, she questioned whether it had been wise. Even the silly coachman would have been protection from the three coach passengers who had been leering at her for most of the afternoon. She was, of course, duly grateful to Lieutenant Redepenning for happening along before they caught up with her. But she had a pistol. She would have managed perfectly well without him.

"I have some rope here," Lieutenant Redepenning was saying, as he looked through his saddle bags. "Ah. Here it is. Pass me the carpet bag, Miss Pritchard, and we'll let the horse carry it the rest of the way to the village."

She rather thought he needed the horse more than the carpet bag did, but arguing with Richard Redepenning had always been an exercise in futility. He was the only person she knew who could out-stubborn her, though that was at least in part because of the pointless *tendre* she had held for him since the first time he had rescued her.

She had been nine years of age, and cross with that year's nurse. She wanted apples for tea, and the nurse told her the country grew no apples. Silly woman. Mary had passed an apple seller in the market earlier that day. No point in taking an appeal to Papa. Papa would no more countenance insubordination within his family than within his crew.

So Mary waited until Nurse was asleep, then crept out of her cabin and set off to find the market.

Which was not at all where she expected it to be. She soon became lost in a maze of little streets, and her red hair and fair skin attracted a forest of locals, looming over her and making incomprehensible sounds, while she stood at bay against a wall and prepared to fight for her life.

Then the crowd melted, and Midshipman Redepenning was there, smiling at her and holding out a hand, all the time talking to the village people in their own language. At fourteen, he had been a beautiful boy, tall and slender, with a crop of golden blond hair and intensely blue eyes.

He didn't growl, or complain about the nuisance of girl children. He didn't suggest that her father beat her (not that Papa ever did). He escorted her home to the ship, and helped her sneak back into her cabin. He even took a detour through the market and bought her an apple.

Mary had fallen in love that day, and she stayed in love as the boy grew to the handsomest, kindest man she knew. No other man ever measured up. Not that Lieutenant Redepenning cared. As far as she could see, he still thought of her as the child that continually needed rescue.

"Miss Pritchard?" There she was lost in memories of some far-off sunny shore, while Lieutenant Redepenning stood in front of her with his piece of rope at the ready.

"Thank you." She hoisted the bag up and balanced it on the saddle while he tied it, with quick efficient sailors' knots. The band box went up next, tied in front of the bag.

"If you would see to the gate, Miss Pritchard?" he suggested. "I can walk well enough, but I'm not as spry as I was."

They slowly sauntered down the hill path, Mary holding the proffered arm but attempting to put no weight on it.

Anxiety made her cross. He shouldn't be walking. Idiot man. He should have stuck to riding, and the road. If he were sore tonight, it would be his own fault. She didn't ask him to follow her.

They came to another gate, and, on the other side, to a bench seat that looked over the village, now almost close enough to touch. The church roof and the top floor of the inn were at eye level.

The last stretch of path, though short, was going to be a problem. It was steep and narrow. How would Mary get the lieutenant down it without injury? She frowned at it with disfavor.

"Let us sit for a minute," she suggested.

He was willing enough, tying the horse to a handy bush and lowering himself to the seat with a sigh.

Best to be frank. "Lieutenant Redepenning, the path is very steep and narrow. How are we to manage it?"

"You used to call me 'Rick'," he observed.

Dear God, how blue his eyes were. That twinkle was just as devastating as ever. What had he said?

Oh, yes. "You used to call me 'Mary'," she retorted. "And how are we to get you down the path, Lieutenant?"

"Rick," he insisted.

"Rick, then." She gave way on that point, but continued to glare. She would not be distracted from her purpose.

"Mary." His voice was a caress, giving her plain name a music it never had. Good heavens, was Rick the Rogue flirting? With her? With Mary Pritchard, the bluestocking, forthright as a sailor and homely to boot? He was just trying to divert her.

Her frown deepened, and she raised one eyebrow.

Rick complied.

"I confess it is a problem. The doctor says the break is knitting well, and I just need to wait for the tissues to recover. It will repair entirely in time, but after a day's riding or much walking, the leg does not obey as it ought. I think if you will lead the horse, Mary, I can lean on the bank and make my way safely down. Shall we rest here a moment, then give it a try?"

Chapter Two

Usually, he hated admitting his weakness. In his own mind, he feared the doctor was wrong about his eventual recovery, and he sometimes wondered if the decision to keep the leg was doing him any favors. Somehow, he didn't mind Mary knowing about the pesky thing.

Perhaps because he knew she wouldn't make a fuss. In London, his male friends had looked away, embarrassed, and his sister and her friends had hovered over him and fussed around till he was ready to scream.

Mary just said, "Very well."

They sat in silence for a few minutes.

Rick broke the silence. "May I inquire about your intended direction, Mary?"

She frowned at him, then looked pointedly away. "Am I in another bumble-broth from which you must rescue me, you mean?"

He smiled back. "Are you? I would be happy to be of service, you know."

"I am no longer nine, thank you, Lieutenant Redepenning." Her voice dripped ice. "I would not at all wish to further inconvenience you."

Miss Mary was in a taking. What had he done to offend her? Rick hazarded a guess. "I called on you in London. Did you know?"

She turned startled eyes to him. "You did? When?" Then, brows drawing together, she asked, "Did my aunt send you to find me?"

So she had run away. "I called several times. Not recently. Not since your aunt told me that you had no wish to see me."

An angry huff of air escaped. "She... I... That..." Mary swallowed whatever words might have finished the interrupted sentences, taking to her feet to march up and down the small, flat ledge, with her lips tightly pressed together, as if to stop any further outburst.

Rick waited. Her angers were sudden, but quickly over. In a few more strides, she would be calm again. How pretty she was, with indignation coloring her cheeks under the light dusting of freckles.

She stopped in front of him, looking down. "Rick, I had no idea you had visited, and I certainly never gave such a message. I would never turn away..." She blushed a little more, and finished,

"…someone who served with my father."

Rick wondered what she first thought to say.

"My aunt takes too much on herself." She fairly quivered with indignation.

He ventured another guess: "And is that why you're here, Mary? Your aunt taking too much on herself?"

Mary didn't answer; not directly. "I am going to Haslemere to live with my Aunt Dorothy and my Aunt Marjery. I find the frivolous life does not suit me." She frowned down at the rooftops. "It is not far, is it?"

He accepted the change of subject, levering himself back to his feet. "Shall we have a go at this path, Mary? I can hear the coachman and his ducklings up on the road above us, and I would like to secure rooms at the inn before they arrive."

Mary and the horse went down the path first. She waited at the bottom, trying not to let her anxiety show as Rick slowly and carefully worked his way from rocky step to rocky step. He was pale and pinched when he reached the bottom, but made a brave attempt at his usual jaunty grin.

"There. That is the worst of it. Lead us to the inn."

They took the last one hundred yards slowly, he leaning at least some of his weight on the horse, she matching her pace to his without comment.

The innkeeper took the news of a stranded coachload of passengers in his stride. "Some of the men will 'ave to double up, sir, but I've a good suite for you and your sister: two bedchambers and a private sitting room." He looked at the two of them suspiciously. "And will Miss Reid's maid be arriving with the others?" Reid was the surname Rick had written in the register.

"My maid, unfortunately, was taken ill and was not able to accompany me," Mary said.

"You should not have gone on without her, sister, dear," Rick scolded. "Fortunately, I was at home to receive your message and was able to follow after you before any harm was done."

My goodness, he sounded exactly like a patronizing older brother. She snapped back, "All would have been well, if the coachman had not landed us in a ditch."

He opened his mouth to say something more, but his leg suddenly gave way, and he lurched, catching her shoulder as she moved to support him, her irritation forgotten.

"Rick, you've overdone things. Oh, dear, I should never have let you walk. Innkeeper, you take his other side, and we'll get him to his room. Oh, dear, why did you not say?"

Together, she and the innkeeper supported Rick up the stairs to a small but comfortable suite, leaving a servant to bring her luggage and Rick's modest saddle bags.

"I just need to sit for a while," Rick insisted. The innkeeper helped him to the room's sofa, where he was able to stretch out the damaged leg.

Mary ordered water for washing, brandy for Rick, and a glass of negus for herself, to be delivered immediately. "And we shall want a hot meal, innkeeper, but that can wait until…" She looked at Rick uncertainly. A lifetime on shipboard had taught her that men needed to be fed regularly, but she also knew that pain suppressed the appetite.

"An hour, perhaps?" Rick suggested. He was lying back on the cushions, his eyes shut.

"An hour," Mary confirmed to the innkeeper. After she had settled on a selection of dishes from those the inn offered, she kept herself busy to avoid thinking about the fact that she was alone with the man they called Rick the Rogue. Not that he'd ever been anything but a gentleman with her. And she was pleased about that. She was.

In the bedchamber allocated to her, she removed her bonnet and turned down her sheets, slipping a hand between them to check for damp. She then set out clothes for the next day, arranged her hair brush and tooth powder on the night stand, rearranged the screen in the corner, and used some of the water a servant brought to wash her face and hands.

She didn't quite dare to enter Rick's room, but she instructed the servant who arrived with the hot water to turn down Rick's bed, and she stood in the doorway while the servant tested the sheets.

"Now put Lieutenant Rede… Lieutenant Reid's bags on the coverlet so he can easily reach them. There."

Rick was propped on the sofa cushions, his brandy cradled in both hands, his eyes still closed. Every few minutes, he would lift the glass and take another sip. She bustled around the small sitting room, moving the fire screen so he wouldn't get too hot, placing a small table conveniently close to

Rick's elbow for his brandy and later his dinner plate, moving a light wing chair for herself, so he could easily see her without turning his head.

When she ran out of things to do, she sat and watched him. He really was devastatingly attractive. For a moment, she let herself dream she had a right to sit here opposite him, studying the planes of his face, the lock of hair that had escaped his ribbon and was teasing the side of his cheek, the broad shoulders in the uniform jacket he had loosened but not removed.

A knock on the door broke her reverie. Dinner. Yes. No more of this nonsense, Mary Pritchard. As if Lieutenant Richard Redepenning, Rick the Rogue, could ever be interested in someone like her!

Chapter Three

What a woman she had grown into! She made Rick comfortable with quiet competence, leaving him to rest until the pain died down to a quiet ache. No fussing. No questions about what she could do for him. She just set the suite to rights and sat peacefully until the meal arrived.

Over dinner, they fell back into the easy habit of conversation they'd enjoyed aboard her father's ship, before Rick had been promoted elsewhere in the fleet.

They disagreed about Russia's trustworthiness as an ally in the long war against France, and agreed that General Bonaparte was a dangerous man, and debated passionately about the wisdom of a reduction in the militia, Mary's color rising to tint her skin pink. Skin so fair as to be translucent, with a soft dusting of freckles across her tip-tilted nose. Her long pale eyelashes glinted in the candlelight as they swept down to brush her cheeks, and her copper curls, as averse to confinement as the rest of her, sprang free of her ribbon as she shook her head at whatever he had just said. What had he said? Lost in totaling her features, he had lost track of his argument.

"You are tired," she decided.

You are pretty, he thought. But she was correct, as well, so he let her chivvy him off to bed.

In the morning, he felt considerably more the thing, and after breakfast, they set off in a hired chaise for Haslemere, where her aunts lived.

"It is on my way, Mary," he told her, and she allowed him to escort her.

They arrived in Haslemere in mid-afternoon, and stopped across the street from the address Mary had been given.

She turned to smile at him, a full Mary Pritchard beam. The smiles of Admiral Pritchard's daughter had been known to melt the heart of the toughest bo'sun, and to turn the crews of an entire fleet into putty in her hands.

"Lieutenant Redepenning, Rick, I cannot thank you enough." She held out her little gloved hand expectantly.

"I will see you inside, of course," he said. And check the aunts were really there, and the place was a safe one for Mary to stay.

"I suppose you will insist." Mary frowned. "I'd hoped to save you from getting down out of the curricle."

He ignored her protests and lowered himself carefully, good leg first, then turned and offered her a gallant hand. Good sailor that she was, she made no fuss, but nor did she put any weight on him as she hopped down to the pavement.

"Let's leave the bags there while we check to see if we have the right place?" Rick suggested. He told the post boy to keep an eye on the bags as well as the horses, before he and Mary crossed the street.

The door was opened almost as soon as he banged the knocker, and they walked into chaos. A bewildering number of maids were running back and forth along the hall. Laden trays appeared from the back of the house, from which delicious smells of spice and baking wafted, then disappeared into the front room to the right. Empty trays were whisked back down the hall, the two processions of maids turning sideways to prevent collisions. A short, plump, elderly woman in an old-fashioned print gown and large, white pinafore stood at the door to the front room, watching all that went on with the eye of a ship's captain.

Rick would have known her in a crowd for the admiral's sister. She had the same light blue eyes, the same determined chin, the same bulbous nose (albeit in a more feminine cast), and the same air of command.

Mary was in no doubt either. "Aunt Dorothy?"

Next moment, she was enveloped in an enthusiastic hug. "Fletcher's little girl. It must be. Darling Mary, let me look at you." The woman held her at arms' length, then pulled her in for another hug. "Why, you are the image of my mama. Did your dear papa ever tell you that? He must have. Just look at you."

Ignoring Rick and the maids, Miss Pritchard proceeded to hug Mary, untie her bonnet, hug her again, help her off with her coat, clucking over her the whole while.

After a few minutes, she seemed to realize she had spectators. "But what am I thinking! Maudie, dear, look after the baking. Mary, come away into the house, and you—Mary's friend—you come too."

Rick excused himself after promising to send in Mary's bags and to visit again tomorrow.

He carried away an image of her looking a little lost. *If she isn't happy with her place when I return,* he vowed, *I'll carry her off and find her a safe berth somewhere else.*

Mary found herself swept along by a sort of a female tempest to the rear of the hall, avoiding the continuing procession of maids as they went. They came to harbor at the end of the hall in a small, cluttered, feminine parlor.

"Now then, Mary, my girl. Tell me what you are doing here, and who that gentleman was. Not that I am not pleased to see you, for that I am, and no mistake, but fetching up on my doorstep with no warning, and in the company of a gentleman, with not even a maid to give you countenance! It needs to be explained, my dear. That it does."

"Aunt Dorothy, that was Lieutenant Redepenning. He served with father, and he was kind enough to escort me from Merroham after the coach broke down."

Aunt Dorothy eyed her thoughtfully. "Hmm, that explains the young man, I suppose, but what were you doing on the coach in the first place?"

Mary blushed a little, and looked at the paintings on the wall rather than her aunt. "I found that London life did not suit me, Aunt. And in your letters, you said I would always be welcome."

"That you are, dear, that you are. Never doubt it. Though if I'd known you were coming... Well, here you are, and I am so pleased to see you, and so Marjery will be." She pursed her lips a little. "And your cousin, Enid, of course." The broad smile returned. "They are making afternoon calls, dear, but will be home soon."

A maid arrived with a large trolley containing a tea service and a plate tower with different types of cakes and tarts on each layer.

Aunt Dorothy busied herself with pouring the tea.

"You will wonder at the bustle here, my dear. We are known for our baking, you know." She puffed herself up, looking for all the world like a contented hen. "We are always called on to supply baking for church fairs, assemblies, and other such things.

And, just think, dear, our baking is much in demand at the market!" She deflated a little. "It is not trade, dear, whatever Enid says. Your cousin is a little sensitive." She shook herself, as if to settle her feathers.

"Now, Mary, tell me the truth. What happened in London? I thought your mother's sister would have found you a husband. Aha! That is it, is it not? She picked someone, and you ran away!"

Chapter Four

After his visit to check on Mary, Rick reluctantly left Haslemere, because he couldn't find a reason to stay. He wasn't family, and Mary was an adult, able to make her own decisions. Rick had no right to interfere with her choices.

That's what this reluctance was; concern she was making the wrong choice. Rescuing Mary Pritchard was the habit of half a lifetime. She was a friend. Just a friend. He wasn't so foolish as to dangle after a girl who showed no awareness of him as a man.

When he called that morning, Miss Pritchard and her sister, Lady Rumbold, had been as protective of her as they should be. Rick couldn't doubt that

Mary was welcome, and that she would be looked after.

Even so, all the way to his father's house in Portsmouth, where he planned to stay for a month, he felt a nagging sense of loss. He kept turning to Mary to tell her something, and she was never there.

The hollow ache didn't go away. It followed him around Portsmouth. He visited with friends. He travelled across to Haslar to see a doctor at the naval hospital who recommended leg-strengthening exercises, which he carried out faithfully several times a day. And all the time he missed Mary.

Papa couldn't get down from London, but he said Rick was to treat the house as his own. The staff had either been ship's crew with Papa or servants at Longford, his boyhood home, when Mama was chatelaine there. Rick had never been better looked after. Or more lonely.

He came home one day from dinner, with a friend who'd just been raised to commander, and who was about to take his new ship to join the fleet in the West Indies. If it hadn't been for a freak gust of wind, it could have been Rick; he was due his own ship. Who knew how many of his friends and colleagues would jump ahead of him while this stupid leg healed?

"There is a letter for you, Lieutenant," said Markham, the butler. "From your sister, I believe."

He pounced on the letter and carried it into the study, where the brandy decanter was waiting on a small table next to his favorite chair. He took a letter opener to the wax seal and was soon settled with his leg up on a footstool, a glass of brandy at hand, and Susan's letter spread before him.

She must be on an economizing drive again. The feminine loops and swirls were tiny, and she'd used every inch of the sheet of paper, writing on both sides, and crossing the horizontal lines of text with vertical lines, and then writing more on the inside and edges of the enveloping sheet.

He deciphered the first page: Susan started with an outline of her social activities, interspersed with news of his baby niece, little Amelia, the only occupant of Susan's nursery. Captain Cunningham, Susan's husband, had been posted to the Far East shortly after Amy's birth, more than four years ago.

Here were a few sentences about their father, who was, Susan said, working long hours at the Horse Guard, but still found time to come and play with his granddaughter.

Ah. Here's what he'd been looking for.

You asked after Admiral Pritchard's daughter. Does this mean you know where she is? For I swear, her aunt does not, though she is putting a good face on it.

After I received your letter, I went to one of the Lady Bosville's afternoons at home. Such a bore, so you owe me the new bonnet you promised me. She does not offer refreshments or any entertainment, so one sits and talks to people one does not know about people one does not like.

Rick frowned as he read on. Susan said it was an open secret that Mary's aunt had been warning off suitors all season, meaning to keep Mary for her son—or Mary's money, more to the point. When

Susan asked after Mary, Lady Bosville claimed she was in the country, recovering from a small cold, and would return soon.

At the Haverford Ball several nights later, Susan had danced with Bosville in order to interrogate him. Rick's frown deepened as he read.

I asked him if it was true that he was betrothed to my friend, Mary, and he said his mama had it all arranged, and he would have to comply because they were near rolled up. He really did. And I a near stranger to him, and like to be more so, I can assure you.

So, I said that she was a sweet thing, and very pretty. Well, he told me that he did not admire pasty skin and red hair, and I would not call her sweet if I had heard her in a temper! But, he said, he could always park her at his country estate, which he never visits, because it is so boring. I know what you are thinking, and I agree with you.

Susan finished with a few trenchant observations about the Bosvilles and a sisterly farewell. After reading her final admonition to follow the doctor's instructions, Rick refolded the letter. His mind was made up. It was time for him to return to London, anyway. And he would do it via Haslemere. He was sure Mary was in safe hands, but he would not rest easy till he saw for himself.

Mary smiled with satisfaction as she placed the last of the little gingerbread ladies into the box. In the four weeks she had been at Aunt Dorothy's, she had learned a number of recipes, and helped with all kinds of baking, but the gingerbread biscuits, which she had learned from the cook on the Olympus, became her specialty.

Making them took her back to the galley where Cook ruled with a rod of iron over various helpers, but always had time for a lonely little girl. She could still hear his deep, gravelly voice telling the story of the runaway gingerbread horse, or it might be a dog, or whatever cutter shape he had used at the time. She would be hovering over the tray of hot biscuits, waiting for them to cool enough to ice and eat.

"And he ran, and he ran," Cook would say, "with all the village behind him: the old lady, the fat squire, the pretty milkmaid, and the hungry sailor. But none of them could catch the gingerbread horse."

The story would continue, with the gingerbread horse escaping one would-be eater after another, and mocking them all, until Cook had iced the first biscuit. Mary would wait, patient and giggling, for the gingerbread horse to encounter the river, and the fox.

First, he'd put the horse over her back. Then, as the river water rose, on her head. And finally, she would tip her head back, and he would perch the biscuit on her nose, and say the words she had been waiting for: "And bite, crunch, swallow, that was the end of the gingerbread horse."

Aunt Dorothy had round and star cutters, and

cutters in the shape of various animals. When the alderman's daughter asked for gingerbread ladies and gentlemen for her wedding breakfast, Mary had been delighted with the notion, and the cutters the tinker made to her pencil drawings worked very well.

The icing gave them clothes and features; a whole box of little gingerbread grooms, and a box of little gingerbread brides. The alderman's daughter would be very pleased with this trial run, Mary thought.

But as she folded tissue over the biscuits to keep them safe, she sighed. She should love it here with her aunts and her cousin. She enjoyed making delicious things to eat. Though Aunt Dorothy and Aunt Marjery thought it improper for her to help at the market, she did join them for meetings with people who were commissioning food for their entertainments, and they were encouraging her to take more and more of a lead in those meetings. For the first time since her father died, she felt she was doing something useful.

And she had company. Although she was currently alone in the small workroom off the kitchen, she could hear the kitchen staff busily working a few feet away. She and her aunts spent much of their time together, though her cousin Enid was often out visiting friends. Aunt Dorothy was as sweet as the confections she made, delighted to have Mary with her, and eager to teach her all about what was clearly a business, though Aunt Dorothy insisted it was merely a hobby.

Aunt Marjery was more reserved, but it was only natural for her to be more interested in her own daughter than a niece who was a stranger, except for a lifetime of letters. Mary got on well with the maids, and it was nice to spend time with women near her own age, though their consciousness of the class difference, and Mary's relationship with their employer, stood in the way of close friendship.

But four things conspired to spoil her enjoyment. First, she missed the sea. She had lived her entire life within the sight, smell, and sound of it, until she first came to London, and as each day passed, she yearned for it more and more. The sea was home, and this land-locked valley, however pretty, was not.

Second, no matter how sharply she spoke to herself, she could not stop thinking about Rick Redepenning. She couldn't possibly miss a man she had spent less than a day with in the past five years. She was merely worried about his injury, that was all, that he might not be taking care, might not be healing. No matter what excuses she made, she was well aware she was in danger of once again falling in love with Rick the Rogue—if, in fact, she'd ever fallen out of love.

Third, Cousin Enid did not want her here. At first, Mary had been sure she was just being over-sensitive, but Enid took every opportunity to find fault and to sow discord between Mary and Enid's mother. And all was done with a smile, with poisonous remarks in a voice that dripped treacle, until Mary doubted she'd heard correctly.

Mary tried to like Enid. They were cousins, after all. But she was impossible to like. She made it clear she did not want to live in this country town, and she resented the enterprise absorbing Aunt Dorothy and distracting Enid's mother, another dumpling of a woman, but a faded shadow of her sister.

Enid would be leaving, she told her mother bluntly, as soon as she had control of her inheritance. That happy day was still some six years in the future, when she turned twenty-five, unless she found a man of suitable rank and wealth to be worthy of her hand in the country backwater in which her mother insisted they remain. Meanwhile, she refused to have anything to do with the baking for fear the taint of 'trade' might follow her into a life better suited to her consequence as daughter of an esquire.

As Mary carefully tied the two boxes of gingerbread ready for delivery, the fourth cause of her discomfort came in.

"Well, hello, Miss Pritchard. All alone, are we? How pretty you look this morning."

The alderman, Mr. Owens, was a regular and popular visitor to the house, so much so, he wandered freely into the kitchen and its attached workrooms without announcement, as he had today. According to the maids, the widower had set his sights on Miss Dorothy Pritchard for his next wife, and she—Mary was convinced—was not averse to the idea. Recently, however, his heavy compliments had been addressed to Mary, and he seemed to go out of his way to find her alone.

She inclined her head, the barest minimum politeness required.

"Have you come to collect your daughter's baking, sir?"

"No, no. Ruthie will do that herself. She's just

out there in the kitchen with your good aunts. What have you there, eh?" He came around the table to her side. As Mary moved backward to avoid him, her head struck the shelf behind her, upending a canister that struck her a glancing blow as it fell. Mary staggered, and was momentarily grateful for Mr. Owens' steadying hands.

Until she heard the gasp from behind him.

Until she opened her eyes to see both aunts, her cousin, and Ruth Owens standing in the doorway, their mouths identical 'O's of shock.

Chapter Five

She should visit her mother's sister, Aunt Theo. That's what Mary told Aunt Dorothy and Aunt Marjery. Like them, Aunt Theo had faithfully written every month of her life, and now that Mary was in England, the least she could do was visit her.

She didn't tell the aunts Enid had suggested she leave town, unless she wished to break Aunt Dorothy's heart.

The aunts had accepted Mary's explanation of what looked like an embrace. Even so, Aunt Dorothy had been looking askance at her suitor since the incident, and Mary didn't want to make more trouble.

Aunt Dorothy and Aunt Marjery raised all kinds of reasons why Mary should stay, but were no match for her determination. However, they put their foot down when it came to Mary's travel.

"Not in a public coach, Mary," Aunt Dorothy said, "and what the viscountess was thinking when she let you travel that way, I do not know. You'll take a post chaise, and Polly from the kitchen shall go with you."

Mary was pleased to be persuaded, and on a fine morning in early December, she and Polly climbed into the yellow bounder for the three-day journey to Oxford, where Aunt Theo lived.

"I wish you would stay for the wedding," Aunt Dorothy said, for the thousandth time.

Mary shook her head. The wedding was later that morning, but Enid and Ruth Owens had made it clear Mary would be unwelcome. "If I leave it much later, I will not be able to go until after Christmas. I will not be missed, Aunt Dorothy, but you have a wonderful time."

Soon, they were on their way. Polly was good company, full of stories about people and activities in the village, and endlessly curious about Mary's travels and adventures. The aunts had packed a huge basket of food, enough for the two women, the post rider, and (Polly joked) a small village of hungry orphans. They nibbled throughout the day, rather than stopping somewhere for a meal.

When Mary ventured a wish that Ruth Owens would have a good day for her wedding, Polly snorted. "Pity poor Thomas Wright, that's what I say. He'll be under the cat's paw, just like her poor father."

"Miss Owens seems very fond of Mr. Wright," Mary ventured.

Polly snorted again. "A cat may be fond of a mouse, I suppose, but that is not a benefit to the mouse, is it, Miss?"

"She will be going to live in Bristol, I understand."

"She wants her da to move to Bristol with them," Polly said. "She was wild as fire when her da started calling on Miss Pritchard. Wants to keep him for herself, and doesn't like Miss Enid above half. Can't be two queens in the same house, and that's a fact.

"Stop him, she will, if she can. But he is stubborn, is Mr. Owens. He will outlast her, I reckon. Just keep on sticking where he is, he will, until she goes off to Bristol, and then he will ask Miss Pritchard to walk out."

"He was very attentive to me," Mary said. What would Polly say to that?

Polly went off into a peal of laughter. "Oh, Miss, you didn't think…? Why, Miss, he told everyone you reminded him of his own Mary, Ruthie's older sister who died. She would be about your age if she lived, Miss. Mind you, Ruthie didn't like that. No, not one bit. Miss Enid used to rub it in ever-so. Not that Miss Enid is good at sharing, either. Now, Miss, how about another of your stories? Did you ever go to one of them islands with the palm trees? Is it true they don't wear hardly any clothes?"

The house was closed for a wedding, one of the elderly gentlemen lounging outside the tavern told Rick. The daughter of one of the local notables was wedding a lawyer's clerk from Bristol, and most of the village was attending.

Rick arranged a room for the night, ordered a jug of the local beer, and found a seat in the sun to wait for the ladies to return home.

The sun was setting when Miss Pritchard's aunts and cousin came up the road, surrounded by a bevy of women brightening the evening in their pretty bonnets and hats. But none were Mary.

Miss Pritchard invited him into her comfortable parlor, where she told him Mary had decided to visit her Aunt Theo in Oxford.

"We sent her off in a post chaise, Lieutenant Redepenning," said Miss Rumbold, the cousin, "so you may be quite comfortable about her safety."

Rick wasn't comfortable, though. After he finished the tea Miss Rumbold insisted on serving him, and made his careful way back across the road to the inn, he sat on the edge of his bed, worrying about all the things that could go wrong when two young women travelled with just a post boy for protection.

He slept poorly, and by morning, he had made up his mind. He would follow Mary to Oxford, and see for himself that she was all right.

Mary was pleased to reach the end of the first

day's travel. She climbed down at the posting inn, stretching the kinks out of her back and knees, as Polly clambered down to join her.

The inn allocated them a pair of rooms on the second floor, near the back, and they were climbing the stairs when they passed someone coming down. He was looking at the gloves he was putting on, rather than where he was going, and Mary had to step smartly to the right to avoid a collision.

He looked up impatiently, saying, "Watch where you are going, Ma—Cousin Mary? Good God, it is. What are you doing in this godforsaken place?"

Lord Bosville. Of all the people Mary imagined meeting, he was the last she'd expect to find this far from London. "Cousin," she replied, giving him a frosty nod. They had parted on unfriendly terms, after he had tried to kiss her and she had, as her father had taught her, punched him in a vulnerable part of his anatomy.

Bosville rearranged his face into a friendly smile that did not reach his eyes. "I do apologize for my language, Cousin Mary. I was startled. How nice to see you. Mother will be delighted to hear you are well. She has been so worried."

What nonsense. Mary suppressed a snort. Worried to have lost Mary's money, perhaps.

"If you will excuse me, Cousin, my maid and I are tired."

But Viscount Bosville turned and accompanied them up the stairs, insisting he would see them safely to their rooms. "And after you are refreshed, dear cousin, you will, of course, allow me the privilege of providing a small dinner? In a private parlor, so you need not hesitate for a moment."

"Thank you, Cousin, but we are very tired…"

Viscount Bosville kept arguing all the way to their rooms, and stood in the doorway, still insisting, until Mary agreed, just to be rid of him.

"Excellent, Cousin. I will do myself the honor of escorting you myself. Shall we say eight o'clock?"

Mary closed the door on him, and wondered how she could gracefully extricate herself from his fulsome and insincere compliments over dinner. Perhaps a sudden and unexpected dose of the plague?

Bosville kept to his side of the table. Mind you, that could be because Mary took Polly down to dinner with her, and showed the viscount the little pistol that Mary always carried for protection.

Even if he wasn't a danger, he was a bore. He couldn't seem to grasp she didn't find him, his friends, and his activities as engrossing as he did. And he seemed to have convinced himself her refusal of his advances was modesty, not repulsion. He said, several times, he realized he had rushed her. He apologized for his haste, but assured her it was her fault for being so beautiful.

Mary, who had heard him describe her to a friend as his homely cousin, was not fooled. Replying in monosyllables, changing the subject, looking all around the room instead of at him; all the little strategies she could try and still stay just this side of good manners, he ignored. He was delighted to carry the full burden of the conversation, ignored any topic she raised, and did not look at her often enough to notice her distraction. As soon as she could, she escaped to bed.

Mary and Polly left the inn before the sun was fully up, to avoid his escort. Mary felt silly. Surely she was overreacting. What could he do, after all? This wasn't medieval times.

Even so, as the post chaise left the inn, and turned onto the Oxford Road, she relaxed. She needn't think about Bosville again.

"Would you care for a game of cards, Polly?"

The morning passed quickly, and in the afternoon, both women fell asleep after finishing the picnic lunch packed by the inn.

Mary woke when the post boy shouted, and all of a sudden, the carriage leapt as it sped up. With difficulty, she pulled herself to the front window. The increased velocity set the carriage lurching and swaying worse than a ship in a storm. The windows were too dirty for easy viewing, but she could see no sign of the post boy, and on either side, the hedges rushed by. The horses must have bolted!

Could she get to the front luggage rack from the side door? If she didn't try, would she and Polly survive?

Balancing herself as best she could, she used her free hand to pull her skirt up from the back to tuck it into her sash, leaving her legs free. She wound one end of a long shawl around her wrist, and gave the other end to Polly.

"Polly, hold tight," she said. Polly, veteran oldest sister of a tribe of boys, wedged herself into the corner of the seat.

When Mary opened the door, it whipped back out of her hands. She caught both sides of the doorway, and then, grasping every handhold she could find, she pulled herself forward up onto the luggage rack. The horses were uncontrolled, galloping heedless and headlong with the post boy nowhere to be seen.

She sent up a quick prayer of thanks that this part of the country had long straight roads, sunk between hedges. In any other carriage, she might have had a chance of grabbing the reins, but this was a post chaise, controlled by the post boy who rode one of the horses. Back here on the carriage itself, there were no reins to grab.

The carriage bounded over a large rut or rock, and she was airborne for a moment, holding the front rail of the luggage rack with a white-knuckled grip. With a thump that jarred every bone in her body and expelled what little breath she had left, she crashed back onto her trunks. She would be safer inside the carriage.

As she edged her way cautiously back to the door, a flash of movement behind the hedge to her left caught her eye. A rider? The hedge thickened again, and she couldn't be sure. Another bounding lurch prompted her to move again, and she swung herself back inside to rejoin Polly—though not without a few extra bruises.

"The post boy is gone, and the horses are

bolting," Mary told Polly. "Stay in your corner and hold on tight. And pray that they run themselves out before we reach a bend in the road."

Following her own advice meant she couldn't see whether the glimpse she'd caught was a rider. Someone riding to their aid would be wonderful, but unlikely. Might as well wish for Rick to save her once again.

Polly, to her credit, didn't panic, just held on grimly, her face white and her lips moving—whether in prayer or cursing, Mary couldn't tell. Mary was praying. This was no time to annoy God!

Were the horses slowing? Yes. They were no longer in a full-out panicked gallop. Quite quickly, the gallop became a canter, and the canter a walk. The horses would be tired, of course. Mary didn't know how long she and Polly had slept, but they must be close to the next posting inn.

She carefully made her way back to the door. Perhaps now that they had slowed, she might be able to do something to stop them?

But there was no need. At the head of the offside horse, shouldering into it with his own horse and pulling the pair to a slower walk and then a stop, was a rider—a rider she recognized.

Rick Redepenning had rescued her again.

Chapter Six

Rick had ridden hard that day, and his leg was complaining bitterly. He'd left Haslemere at first light, making haste along the road to Oxford, compelled by an impulse he didn't understand. He'd lunched at the inn where Mary spent the night, and been alarmed to hear about Viscount Bosville's presence—and Bosville's departure not long after Mary.

He had no cause for concern, surely? Mary was not alone, and this was the end of the eighteenth century, not the middle ages.

Nevertheless, he called for a fresh horse and pressed even harder on Mary's trail.

They were clearly in no hurry. Two more posts later, he was only an hour behind them. This was the last post of the day. He'd see them at the next inn, if he didn't catch up with them beforehand.

Half an hour later, he crested a slight rise, and they were in sight ahead of him on the long straight road, toy-sized in the distance. He narrowed his eyes. What were those men on the side of the road doing? Throwing something?

Several somethings, and the horses reacted, moving from an amble to a panicked gallop in a stride. Rick urged his own horse to a gallop. Pray God the post boy could pull them up! No. There was the post boy, sitting on the side of the road rubbing his head. The assailants had disappeared. Rick didn't have time for them, anyway, and the post boy would have to fend for himself.

Somewhere, off in a compartment of his brain, was the urge to beat the stone throwers, to wail to the sky his fear for Mary. He allowed the emotions to lend him strength and separate him from his pain, but he had no time to pay further attention. Mary needed him.

His best chance was to leave the road; something galloping from behind would panic the team even more. If he could come up beside them, he might have a chance.

He set the hired horse at the first gate he saw, and thanked all the powers of heaven that the beast had a jump in it. More than one, for it gamely soared over several stone walls and hedgerows as they slowly gained on the post chaise.

In glimpses, as the ground on his side of the hedge rose, or as the hedge thinned, he saw his quarry. What was Mary doing? Climbing onto the luggage compartment at the front of the carriage? Did she have any idea how dangerous that was? Of course she did, but he'd be a fool to expect her to wait patiently in an out-of-control chaise bounding towards disaster. It was like her to climb out to see what she could do. She must have concluded there was nothing, for she edged backwards and disappeared again, but not before his brain had recorded an image of her legs that he knew would keep him awake many a fevered night.

Idiot. This was no time for lust. He needed a gate or a low point to get back onto the road at the horses' heads.

There. His horse was tiring, but gathered itself for one more effort and cleared the gate, with a jarring stumble on the other side. He ignored the effect of the sudden lurch on his leg, as he had ignored it on previous jumps, and urged the horse forward. Moments later, he had the bridle of the offsider and was urging the team to a halt.

He looked back at the carriage in time to see Mary jump down from the door, and couldn't help noting she'd dropped her skirts back to where they belonged. He dismounted, taking care to keep hold of the carriage horses, as she hurried towards him.

"Rick, I'm so pleased to see you. What happened to the post boy, do you know? What spooked the horses? What are you doing here?"

Now that the immediate danger was over, his leg hurt like hell. He opened his mouth to reply, but the world spun around him, and he clutched his horse's neck to stay upright.

"Polly, take their heads." Through a haze of pain, he could hear Mary taking over, and suddenly she was under his arm on his better side, supporting him. "I have you, Rick. Just a step. Here, and another."

"A minute," he gasped. "It's jarred. The leg. Not ready for jumping. Good horse, though."

Mary lowered him onto the slope at the side of the road, and was gone. He missed her. She felt good tucked into his side, his arm around her shoulders.

Then she was there again, holding his head against her chest with one hand while she held something to his mouth with another. His mouth flooded with brandy from the flask he carried in his saddle bag.

"Just stay still, Rick. You will be fine in a minute." She sounded calm and confident, but for the edge of a question in the last few words. Brave girl. He had always been able to count on Mary in a crisis.

He took another sip of brandy. Not too much. He would have to ride the horses to the nearest inn, though how he would mount, he had no idea.

Mary would not allow it.

"You will ride in the chaise, Rick, and I will have no argument. You are in no fit state to ride, and I will not have you hurting yourself more on my account. Besides, a fine mess Polly and I would be in if you fell off and the horses spooked again."

"Someone has to ride the horses," he protested.

"I will do it. Just to the nearest farmhouse, so you need not worry for me, Rick."

"Aye, aye, Captain," he managed, which made

her smile, but didn't banish the anxious wrinkle between her brows.

Chapter Seven

Mary entered the bedroom she had commandeered on Rick's behalf, her brow furrowed with concern.

"The doctor thinks the leg is just bruised," Rick told her, "and I have done no further damage."

Her face cleared, and she rewarded him with a beaming smile.

"Was the post boy hurt?" he asked. He had heard Mary marshalling the troops when they arrived at the farmhouse: bargaining with the farmer's wife for bedchambers, sending the farmer's son galloping for a doctor from the nearby town, and instructing others to go back along the road to hunt for the post boy.

"They did not find him. I cannot understand why he did not follow after the horses. Do you think he was confused?"

"Perhaps. Perhaps he went for the constables."

"Yes. You said that some people threw rocks, deliberately frightened the horses. Do you think they meant to kill us, Rick?"

Rick avoided a direct answer. "When you and Polly go on to the inn, make sure you take some of the farmer's men to protect you."

"Go?" Mary put a hand on each hip and frowned. "We are going nowhere until you are fit to travel. Did you think we would leave you? Besides, I have told the farmer's wife you are my brother. A fine sister I would be to leave while you are bedridden!"

"But, Mary…"

"No, Rick, I will not leave you." She gave a decisive nod, her lips firmly pressed together. He sank back against the pillows, too tired and sore to fight her. At least she had claimed to be his sister, which should be some sort of protection to her reputation.

Her stubborn glare dissolved into concern.

"Oh, Rick, here I am brangling with you when you have been injured on my account. No more. I will not leave, but nor will I bother you with arguments."

She made sure he could reach the glass on the bedside table, plumped his pillows, and straightened his blankets. "By the way, our name is Reid, as it was that night on the way to Haslemere. You are

Lieutenant Rick Reid, and I am Mary Reid. I hope you do not mind?"

Good girl. She had thought of everything. With a false name, the fiction they were brother and sister, and her maid to keep her company, she should come out of this with an unscathed reputation. If ever she accepted his suit, he wanted it to be her choice, not something she was forced to do.

The thought startled him awake. Was he courting Mary Pritchard? It seemed he was, the decision made without him knowing it and firmly lodged in his mind. He settled himself more comfortably, his leg now just a dull ache, and fell asleep wearing a smile.

The following morning, Mary sent a message to the posting inn, telling them what had happened and asking for a postilion to present himself, so they could continue their journey.

Rick insisted he had slept and was well enough to travel, though his heavy-lidded eyes suggested an untruth. He insisted on dressing, the farmer's son acting valet, and came down to breakfast, white under his tan and moving stiffly, but refusing to acknowledge weakness.

The postilion was slow arriving, but by mid-morning, they were all in the post-chaise, Rick and Mary sharing the bench seat while Polly sat on a small seat that folded down from the front wall.

Polly was shy at first, but soon the three of them were chatting away, Mary just as enthralled by

Polly's and Rick's tales of growing up in England as Polly was by Rick's and Mary's stories of their journeys and the places they'd seen.

By the time they stopped for a bite to eat in the early afternoon, Rick's pallor had increased alarmingly, and he'd been clenching the front of the bench for more than an hour, his knuckles white with the force of his grip.

He managed a slow, awkward descent from the carriage and twisted his mouth into a shadow of his usual jaunty grin when he caught Mary's concerned frown.

"I'm feeling a bit battered, Mary, but no harm done."

Mary felt a bit battered herself. The carriage was not called a bounder for nothing.

"Let us take our meal in the garden, so we can stroll a little," she suggested, "unless… should you be sitting down, Rick? Or lying even? We could enquire about a room."

"A walk would be just the thing," Rick assured her.

Mary sent Polly off to order sustenance. "We will eat in the garden, Polly. I can see tables under the trees. Order for three. You'll eat with us."

Rick opened the gate from the inn-yard to the garden, and Mary went through it on his arm, trying to support him as much as she could without being obvious.

Another guest was before them, sitting at one of the tables and staring disconsolately at the small, dirty pond that adorned one corner.

"What is the matter?" Rick asked. Mary realized

she had halted and was clutching his arm in a death grip. She willed herself to relax.

"Nothing. It was a surprise to see him here, that was all." Before she could explain herself, the man at the table turned to the sound of their voices, then leapt to his feet and hurried towards them.

"Cousin Mary! You're safe! I'm so..." He stopped just short of them and started again. "Hello, Cousin Mary, what a surprise to see you here. I had thought you at your aunt's already."

He was not looking at Mary any more, but had fixed Rick with a hard stare, which Rick was returning full measure. Any moment, Mary fancied, they'd start snarling and circling.

"Viscount Bosville, may I make known to you Lieutenant Redepenning? Lieutenant, my cousin, Viscount Bosville."

"I know your cousin, George," Bosville said.

"Of course you do," Rick replied.

Bosville, whose color was already high, flushed still more. "He is a good man, is George. Good *ton*."

"No doubt you think so." Rick knew Cousin George to be a rakehell and a bounder.

Bosville, his nostrils flaring, decided on another point of challenge. "Cousin Mary, whatever are you doing alone at an inn with a gentleman? I know you have had... an unusual upbringing, but Lieutenant Redepenning is from a good family. He should know better. You will come with me, Cousin Mary, and we will see what we can salvage of this situation."

Did Bosville realize he had just insulted her family? Mary wondered whether to laugh or hit him, and decided to do neither. "Lieutenant Redepenning and I are about to eat, Cousin. You will excuse us, I am sure."

Bosville drew himself up to his full height, a full head shorter than Rick. "Cousin Mary, I demand you come with me. You have no idea of the damage…"

"No damage," Rick said, moving in so he was looming over Bosville. "Miss Pritchard has been accompanied by her maid at all times, since before she honored me by accepting my escort. Besides, she has been recognized only by her cousin, who will, I am sure, not speak a word of the encounter, nor even think a slur on the lady's reputation."

Bosville took a step back, but said, "Maid? I see no maid."

"Miss Pritchard?" Polly, as if summoned by Bosville's disbelief, appeared at Mary's elbow. "They do a good bread here, they do. And oxtail soup, I thought, if it pleases you. Thick, it is, like your aunt makes, Miss. And a lardy cake too, and cheese and fruit."

"That sounds excellent, Polly," Mary told her. "Cousin, if you will excuse us."

Rick held a chair for her, and then for Polly, eliciting a disgusted snort from Viscount Bosville.

"Really, Redepenning, you should know a maid doesn't sit with her mistress."

Polly, looking distressed, made to stand, but Mary put out a hand to stop her. "Stay where you are, Polly. Really, Cousin Bosville, I certainly cannot eat in public without a companion."

"As your nearest male relative…" Bosville began.

Mary interrupted, "No sermons before our meal,

Bosville, I beg you. Ah, here it is now."

A procession of servants from the inn brought the dishes Polly had mentioned, plus fresh butter, dishes of pickled red cabbage and pickled onions, a plate of pork pies, and jugs of cider and beer.

Bosville watched, clearly trying to decide what to do next. Mary ignored him. Any hope he might just go away was dashed when he pulled out the remaining chair at the table.

"Dashed if I won't join you. You do not mind, do you, Cousin?" He sat without waiting for an answer, and helped himself to a wedge of bread and a mug of beer.

"So, Redepenning," he began. "How do you happen to be travelling with my cousin?"

"It is my privilege to escort Miss Pritchard," Rick said.

"Lieutenant Redepenning saved our lives, and so he did," Polly said, nodding to emphasize her words. "Broken to pieces, that's what would have happened, if he hadn't stopped them horses."

Mary prepared to defend Polly from Bosville's fire. He was outraged at a servant eating with them; surely, he would be furious she dared to speak? But Bosville just looked away, meeting no one's eyes and shifting uncomfortably. "Horses bolted, did they?"

Surely Bosville wouldn't have... She and Rick exchanged glances. He had the same thought, clearly.

"They were deliberately spooked," Rick said. "Know something about that, Bosville?"

His eyes darting everywhere, resting nowhere, Bosville protested. "What do you mean? I don't know anything. What could I know? Ridiculous accusation, Redepenning. Why, I wouldn't hurt a hair on Miss Pritchard's head. I was nowhere near. Word of a gentleman. And if the post boy says different, he lies."

Rick was on his feet, suddenly all hard edges, the cheerful companion submerged in the dangerous warrior. "You fool. Miss Pritchard and her maid could have been killed. What did you plan to do? Ride up and claim the hero's reward? What stopped you? Did your horse throw you?"

Bosville flushed bright red. "Nonsense. Absolute rubbish. You have no proof. None at all. Never meant the chit any harm. Word of a gentleman." As he spoke, he abandoned the table and started backing towards the gate to the inn's yard. "Goodness. Is that the time? Must take my leave, Cousin. You are in good hands with Redepenning. Earl of Chirbury's cousin. Your servant, Cousin. Word of a gentleman. Your servant, Lieutenant."

He reached the safety of the gate and disappeared from sight, obviously fearing that Rick was about to pursue and dismember him.

Mary, though, saw the gray edge of pain at the corner of Rick's lips. "He is gone, Rick. Sit down before you fall," she said.

"That swine. You heard him, Mary. I should strangle him with his own entrails, the stupid, lily-livered cockroach."

"Yes, I heard." Mary supported Rick from his good side, as he lowered himself into his chair, then sat back down next to him. "How did you know what he meant to do, Rick?"

"I was guessing," Rick admitted. "But I was right. You saw him, Mary. He as much as admitted he paid the post boy—and, I imagine, the rock-throwers—to frighten the horses so he could rescue you from a runaway carriage."

Rick's anger was gratifying. He must be a little fond of her, surely?

"I think he meant it when he said he did not mean for me to be hurt. He was genuinely pleased to see me when we first arrived."

How did a man so fair manage to look so dark? Rick's face was a thundercloud. "I daresay he was sorry he'd lost his chance at your fortune," he growled.

Chapter Eight

That might not be the most stupid remark Rick had made in his lifetime, but it was certainly in the top ten. Mary closed up like a tulip at night. He knew what she was thinking: that Rick, like Bosville, thought her fortune was her main attraction. He even knew how to convince her he thought nothing of the kind.

But his hands were tied. She was alone with him, with only the dubious protection of her maid. It would be unconscionable to begin to court her in such circumstances. In all honor, he had to hold her at a distance until he returned her to her family. No matter that he wanted to take her in his arms and kiss her until the fire sparking under her chilly surface flared up to consume them both.

In truth, he was not up to much kissing, and certainly not anything more than kissing. He'd strained the deuced leg again, and would be paying for it the next sennight, undoubtedly. Six months before he could return to the sea, the doctors had said. He hoped this latest strain would not delay his recovery.

Mary's aunt and her husband invited Rick to stay with them in their large rambling house in the countryside, just outside of Oxford.

"This place is much too big, now that all the children have flown," the aunt insisted. "It will be delightful to have young people under our roof again, will it not, Eustace?"

This proved to be an exaggeration: young people trooped in and out of the house all hours of the day. Rick soon found that Dr. Wren, though he had given up his fellowship when he married thirty years or more ago, was much in demand as a tutor. Mrs. Wren, Mary's Aunt Theodora, mothered a large and constantly changing horde of young men and their sisters, and their sisters' friends.

Everyone was full of plans for the Christmas party they would hold in just a few days, before most of them departed for family celebrations. Some, however, would stay on.

"We have eight children, dear," Mrs. Wren explained, "and some of them are too far away to come home for Christmas. I'm happy to give a little love to some other mother's child, and perhaps someone else is doing the same for mine."

They looked an ill-assorted pair: tall, thin, and elegant Mrs. Wren, and short and dumpy Dr. Wren. Her tidy afternoon gown was a triumph of understated elegance, but Dr. Wren might have been wrestling in the clothes he wore under the open academic gown. The gown, too, sat half on and half off his shoulders, and his Tudor cap tilted insecurely on his balding head.

But the connection between the two was palpable, she catching his eye and smiling at the end of every sentence, he watching her over the top of his spectacles, with a twinkle that seemed to approve of whatever she wished to say.

Rick was barely able to move the day after they arrived, but he lay on the couch in a sun room off the Wrens' parlor, where he could join in or rest, as he needed, simply by asking for the connecting doors to be opened or closed.

Mary organized the room for his comfort: a jug of iced tisane close to his elbow, a jar of biscuits, in the unlikely case he became hungry between the large meals Mrs. Wren produced at regular intervals, a rug for his knees, several books, the day's newspaper, and writing materials, so he could catch up on correspondence. Her attentions never bothered him the way his sister's had. Mary didn't fuss. She just got on with the job of making sure he had whatever he needed.

At first, apart from checking from time to time to see all was well, she left him to rest, but when he complained that he lacked company, she turned the room into a gathering place for the visitors, and he found himself discussing philosophy with an undergraduate, arguing naval strategy with another, and playing chess with a disconcertingly clever young woman who trounced him soundly but was magnanimous enough to suggest his leg might have been a distraction.

Chapter Nine

On the following day, he was up and about again, but still found it impossible to get Mary alone. Indeed, she seemed always to be leaving a room as he entered it, and when he tried to follow, good manners required him to stop and attend to whichever person she'd sent to ask his opinion, challenge his beliefs, invite him to a game, or otherwise distract him. He grew sick of hearing, from one person after another, "Lieutenant, Miss Pritchard says…"

So it continued, a cat-and-mouse game that Mary appeared not to notice, and the Wrens watched with benign amusement. He was well enough now to continue on to London, but somehow, he couldn't bring himself to leave.

On Friday night, several days after he arrived, and only a few days before Christmas, they sat fifteen for dinner. It was cheerful, loud, and not at all decorous. People talked across the table, and several were participating in more than one conversation. Dr. Wren was holding his own in a debate about whether Lancelot was a later addition to the Arthurian canon or an original round table member under another name, while simultaneously sharing recipes for mead and arguing about a point in mathematics that Rick nearly understood.

Farther down the table, a group of young ladies were proposing ideas for setting up a dance floor in the garden, since no room in the house could accommodate dancing, as well as the number of guests who would be at the Christmas party on the twenty-third. The chief problem, it seemed, was providing sufficient light so the dancers could see, without setting fire to the trees.

The house would be full on the night of the party, with those staying for Christmas arriving early, and those leaving for home waiting till the next morning. Rick had already told Mrs. Wren he'd move to one of the Oxford inns ahead of the festivities.

The butler, who was really a general factotum, came to stand between Dr. Wren and Rick, and bent over so he would be heard above the hubbub. "Doctor, your nephew, Viscount Bosville, has arrived."

Rick turned to look at the door. Sure enough, the blackguard was there, studying the noisy dinner table with a barely concealed sneer.

"Theo," Dr. Wren bellowed, silencing the guests. "Theo, young Bosville is here for a visit. What do you want to do with him?"

Mrs. Wren went to greet her nephew. The guests took up their conversations, so Rick couldn't hear what she said. In any case, he was watching Mary struggle to maintain an expression of benign indifference.

What the hell was Bosville after? As if Rick didn't know. He toyed with the idea of telling the Wrens what Bosville had done, but he had no proof, and, after all, the man was their nephew.

That settled that. He could not leave now. However she might feel about it, Rick was sticking to Mary. Limpets would be amateurs, compared to Rick, for as long as Bosville stayed in this house.

Chapter Ten

Mary spent the morning dodging Bosville; successfully, thanks to several timely interventions. She was in the dining room near the front door, helping to decorate for tomorrow's party when Cousin Enid arrived.

As if Cousin Bosville were not enough.

"I do beg your pardon for coming unannounced," she heard Enid say. "But my mama was so worried about our dear Mary, after we heard that the coach nearly crashed. And we are such dear friends, Mary and I…"

Mary's hands stilled on the ribbon she was tying around a kissing bough. The lying cow!

Aunt Theo answered, her voice too low for the words to be understood.

"Oh, thank you. I would love to stay, if you are sure it will be no trouble. Why! Lieutenant Redepenning! Are you still here? I had no idea… How delightful."

"Miss Rumbold." Rick sounded politely bland, the voice he used when he wished he were somewhere—anywhere—else. She'd often heard him use it, though, come to think of it, never with her.

They moved away from the door, Enid chattering gaily about how happy she was to see Oxford—"so beautiful, just as I'd heard"—and how pleased she was that Lieutenant Redepenning was back on his feet.

Mary tugged the ribbon with such unnecessary force, it knotted, and she could not unravel it. "Such dear friends," was it? Well, if Enid Rumbold thought to catch Rick Redepenning in her marital claws, she could think again.

Over the noon meal, without a word being said, Mary and Rick joined in a mutual defense pact. Bosville circled, but was deflected with by a sharp glare from Rick. Enid fluttered her eyelashes madly, but desisted when Mary asked, "Why, Enid, darling, do you have something in your eye? Come to the kitchen, and I'll help you wash it."

Bosville tried to enlist Aunt Theo. "Seems like the lieutenant is well enough to move on and stop taking advantage of you, Auntie."

"Lieutenant Redepenning is welcome to stay as long as he wishes, Bosville," Aunt Theo told him.

"We enjoy his company."

"We like invited guests," Uncle Wren added, with a frown.

As at every other meal in the Wren household, an assorted group of people who happened to be in the house at the time sat to eat, but didn't stop the conversations about the projects or activities that brought them to visit.

Bosville had already repelled all attempts at familiarity, and was now being ignored, but the assembled young people were generously willing to include Enid in their conversation.

Their friendly overtures were unsuccessful. Enid had no opinion on water wheel systems for lock construction, or whether Merlin's real name was Myrddin, or the best translation for the Greek word paidiskê. When Mary suggested that women should be allowed to attend lectures at the university, Enid was invited to give her thoughts on the vigorous debate. She batted her eyelids at Uncle Wren, "How dreadful. As if any real woman would want to know about such unladylike things. Oh, but of course, Mary was raised on a navy ship. Very hard to be a lady in such circumstances. I do feel badly for you, Cousin."

Uncle Wren frowned at Enid, and then deliberately turned a shoulder to her. "May I pass you the soup, Mary, my dear?"

Despite the snubs, the two unwelcome guests persisted. Mary avoided them by retreating to the kitchen to make gingerbread shapes—stars, bells, holly leaves, hearts, and ladies and gentlemen, using the cutters the tinker had made for her. She would ice them in the morning.

Aunt Theo knocked on the door just before she hopped into bed. "May I have a moment, my love?"

"Of course, Aunt Theo. Polly, off you go to bed. I won't need you again tonight. Is anything wrong, Aunt?"

"Just those two cousins, my dear. I am sorry that you are so bedeviled. Dr. Wren wishes to toss them both out, but we can hardly send Miss Rumbold out the door when she has travelled three days to be here, and if I cast Bosville into the night not a day before Christmas, my sister will be most offended."

"Oh, Aunt, I do not expect you to do that."

"Just be careful, my dear," Aunt Theo warned. "Do not be alone with my nephew, and do not leave your poor lieutenant alone with Miss Rumbold."

Mary blushed scarlet. "He is not my lieutenant, Aunt Theo."

Her aunt just smiled. "He will be if you want him, dear." With that, she left Mary to her dreams.

Chapter Eleven

When Mary came down to breakfast the following morning, Uncle Wren was there, deep in a conversation with Rick about the kinds of ships that might have been available to King Arthur in defense of his realm. Mary smiled.

Rick, who was looking her way, stumbled over his sentence.

"I am sorry, sir," he said to Uncle Wren, "I have forgotten what I was saying."

Uncle Wren gave him, and then Mary, a benevolent smile. "Well, it does not matter, young man. I have suddenly thought of some correspondence I must to attend to. Will you excuse me?"

As soon as they were alone, Rick crossed to Mary. She looked up into his vivid blue eyes. Could such a magnificent man possibly want her, plain Mary Pritchard?

"Mary." His smile was warm, and his voice, when he said her name, purred along all her nerve endings. A caress in a single word.

"Rick." She tried to match him, and, judging from his sharp intake of breath and the flare in his eyes, was not a total failure.

Then Enid arrived, followed closely by Bosville, and Mary could not help but believe they were up early just to annoy her.

As the morning wore on, she became convinced of it. Bosville was everywhere she turned, and Enid, too, though Mary blamed that on Rick's constant attendance. Enid had clearly decided Rick was to be the next victim of her charm, and was pouring it out with such a lavish hand that Rick looked decidedly ill.

All three even followed her to the kitchen and watched her decorate her gingerbread biscuits with boiled icing and bits of dried fruit.

Mary was grateful to escape on a brief shopping excursion with Polly, slipping out the kitchen door to avoid company, though if she'd been able to attract Rick's attention without alerting Enid's, the walk would have been even more pleasant.

She could not see Rick when she arrived back and delivered the reels of ribbon her aunt had needed. Bosville was there, instructing a bemused undergraduate on the correct tying of a cravat. Enid had finally found common ground with one of Aunt Theo's daughters, vigorously discussing how to attach the swags of evergreen, ribbons, and bells to the picture rail of the main parlor.

When Mary went upstairs to take off her bonnet and pelisse, though, Enid came too. "Mary," she said, "I found something I want to show you. Come this way."

Mary, curious, if a little cautious, followed behind, out the side door and into the garden. "What is it, Enid?" Enid said nothing, just lead Mary down a path until they came around a hedge, and there before them was a small tower, perhaps as tall as the house, but less than ten feet in diameter.

"How charming," Mary said. "What is it for?"

"I have no idea," Enid said, "but I found it yesterday when I walked this way, and I remembered it when you mentioned the dance floor. Wouldn't lanterns up there by the window light this part of the garden?"

It could work. Mary opened the door with some difficulty, because it was stiff, and stepped inside. The tower was hollow, and blank walled until just below the roof, where a series of window spaces let light in. They could easily also let light out, but getting a lantern up could be tricky. Though she could see some possible handholds and footholds…

At that moment, the door shut behind her with a tired groan and then a thud. Shut and—from the sound of it—bolted.

She called out, but Enid was gone, and Mary was well out of earshot of anyone else in the house. What was Enid up to? No good, that was certain. Mary frowned. She would not let her cousin get away with it.

She examined the inner wall of the tower again. Moments later, she'd stripped off her dress and petticoat and was climbing the wall in her stays and under-drawers. It was as tricky a climb as she expected, and Enid was out of sight by the time she reached the windows.

Now what? The outside of the tower was smooth, and besides, she could not climb in the open air in nothing but her undergarments.

Rick came into view, entering the garden through the gate from the road. She smiled. He must have found a way to elude the two cousins and followed her. What a pity she came back the other way.

The next moment, she frowned again. Bosville appeared from the direction of the house, and approached Rick. A few moments of conversation and Bosville handed Rick something—a note, it looked like—clapped Rick on the shoulder, and went off.

Rick stood there, reading the note. He frowned at the path that led down the garden, and then back at the house, clearly suspicious.

Whatever those two were up to, it was time to stop it. Mary, with some effort, managed to push out the ornamental trellis that blocked the window. As it crashed to the ground, Rick stopped in his tracks, looked up at the tower, then turned and went hurrying back towards the house.

Bother. Was she going to have to rescue herself? But as she thought that, the top legs of a ladder appeared. Looking over the side of the tower, she saw Rick holding the ladder steady.

"Your stair awaits, fair princess," he joked.

Dressed, or rather undressed, as she was? She looked back at the inside wall. Perhaps she could climb back down, and he could let her out. But she'd only just made the climb, and her arms were still trembling; she wasn't sure she could get back.

Rick was looking anxious. "Is there a problem?"

"Shut your eyes, please?"

His face cleared. "Of course." And he screwed his eyes shut, rather more dramatically than she thought necessary.

The ladder made the descent easy, and she breathed a sigh of relief as first one foot, then the other, reached the ground. She stopped breathing altogether when Rick's arms came round her waist.

"Do you have any idea what it does to me to see you clambering around a roof, Mary Pritchard?" he asked, holding her so tight she squeaked. He didn't release her, but, instead, bent his head to rub his cheek on her hair. "I'm confident you had an excellent reason, but I swear, I've aged ten years in the last five minutes."

She had had a reason, but for the moment, it escaped her. "Rick?" she asked.

He let her go, stepping backwards. "I beg your pardon. For a moment I... I take it you didn't send the note your nasty cousin gave me?"

He pulled it from his pocket and handed it to her.

"Dear Rick," she read, "please meet me in the summerhouse. With all my love, Mary."

Mary saw red. "That weevil," she hissed. "That sneaky, mean, two-faced little maggot!"

Rick caught her around the waist again before

she could storm down the path. "Whoa, Mary. Who is a maggot? Not Bosville, I take it?"

"Him, too," she fumed. "They're both in on it. Enid locked me in the tower, and Bosville gave you the note."

"Ah," Rick nodded. "Husband-hunting. I thought that might be it. You want to tell them what you think of them, I take it? You might want to get dressed first."

Mary felt the heat of her blush, but Rick the Rogue barely looked her way. He opened the tower door and waited outside while Mary changed.

Chapter Twelve

Rick needed the time on his own to recover. Mary felt every bit as good in his arms as he had imagined, and her state of undress disclosed a shapely form, to which the high-waisted fashions did not do justice. Thinking about the blush that had covered every inch of skin he could see, and clearly carried on where he desperately wished to see, was not helping him calm himself.

Think of something else. Anything. Ah. Here was the perfect distraction—Bosville, rounding the corner and stopping to gape at Rick, the tower, the ladder, and again at Rick.

"What are you doing here?" he asked.

"Waiting for Miss Rumbold, Bosville. She is in the tower, but I'm expecting her to join me."

"But… but my cousin, Mary…"

Rick chose to take that as a question. "Miss Pritchard? She went that way." He pointed down the path.

Bosville opened, then shut, his mouth and hurried away down the path.

Moments later, several other people rounded the house: Dr. and Mrs. Wren and several of the students. "Come along, Theo," said Dr. Wren impatiently. "That young pup insisted on us seeing the surprise in the summerhouse."

Rick and a somewhat-rumpled Mary joined on the tail of the group, and arrived at the summerhouse to find Miss Rumbold in Bosville's arms, her dress drooping to display a naked shoulder and quite a lot of her chemise.

"What, young Bosville, is the meaning of this?" demanded Dr. Wren.

"She just… I just…" Bosville glared at Miss Rumbold in a far from lover-like manner. Clearly, she had decided a viscount in the hand was worth more than a cautious sailor in the bush. "What Lord Bosville is trying to say, Dr. Wren, Mrs. Wren, is that he has asked for my hand in marriage, and I have accepted."

"That isn't… that is to say…" Bosville started, but Dr. Wren shook his hand, Mrs. Wren kissed them both and said she would write immediately to Bosville's mother, and the students declared tonight's Christmas celebration should also be a betrothal party.

"Bosville does not look happy," Rick whispered to Mary.

"How awful Enid is," Mary replied. "I don't like cousin Bosville, but to trap him!"

"They intended to trap us both," Rick pointed out. "They were in it together. She locked you in the tower, and he sent me to the summerhouse."

He had little sympathy for the viscount, and even less as the day wore on. Bosville, at least, had secured a bride, if not the one he intended, but Rick couldn't find even a moment alone with Mary.

She was everywhere, always busy, always in company. More of the Wren offspring arrived, with spouses and children, all delighted to meet Mary, the cousin whose letters from far-flung places had enlivened their lives for many years. She was in demand in the kitchen, where she was making and icing gingerbread shapes for the party supper. She was involved in the last of the decorating.

He gave up, and decided to move his baggage to the inn where he was booked for the night.

"Rick? Are you leaving?" Mary. She stopped in the parlor doorway.

"I'll be back for the party, Mary, but I'll leave from the inn in the morning. My father expects me in London tomorrow night. Mary? Will you walk into Oxford with me?"

Just then, Mrs. Wren and two of her daughters came down the stairs.

"Mary, dear, would you help with the kissing bough in the garden? Lieutenant Redepenning, you're off to the inn? What time do you expect to be back, dear?"

Rick gave some kind of an answer, watching

Mary slip away from him again, carried off by her cousins.

Tonight. At some point tonight, he would find her alone, if he had to carry her off into a dark corner of the garden across the dead bodies of all her relatives.

Rick wanted to see her alone, and Mary had a fair idea why. He thought he'd compromised her when he helped her out of the tower, and he wanted to do the honorable thing. Mary wasn't having it. Enid might be satisfied to trap a husband, but Mary would rather stay single all her life than be married to someone reluctant to have her. Not that Bosville was reluctant anymore. Someone—Enid probably—had told him about Enid's trust fund, and he was as happy as a dog with two tails.

Mary wished them well. She did. But if Rick insisted on proposing, she would turn him down, even though it would break her heart. How she wished he wanted her. For a while, she had hoped... but he had said nothing.

She made her way back to the kitchen. Baking always made her feel better, and gingerbread brides would be a fine betrothal addition to tonight's Christmas party.

The kissing boughs had all been hung, making it perilous to traverse the house and garden. By the time the party started, Mary had been kissed at least twenty times, all polite salutes on the cheek.

The party spilled all over the house and beyond:

carols around the pianoforte in one of the parlors, silly games in another, a continual feast in the dining room, and dancing outside in the crisp night air. Mary managed to avoid being alone with Rick until almost the end of the evening, when he cornered her in a temporarily deserted parlor, most of the party out on the dance lawn in the garden.

"Mary." There it was again. Her name, hummed in that beautiful voice of his, sounding like music. She turned her face upwards, tipping her cheek within easy reach, but he curved his neck as he bent, so that his lips touched hers.

They felt warm and soft and so gentle; as light as a feather, brushing along her mouth as if they would flutter past, then returning to settle. She stood frozen, all consciousness focused on the point of connection. Persuasive lips grazed against hers, until she responded, softening against him.

He moved closer then, sliding his hands around her waist. His mouth opened, and his tongue swept along her lower lip. Startled, she drew back, and he let her go, though his eyes clung to hers.

"Mary, dear Mary, may I…?"

"Don't, Rick, please?" After that kiss, her wits were scattered to the four corners of the garden. All she knew was that she didn't want to hear him propose. She couldn't bear to say no to him, and she had to.

"Rick, I know what you want to say, and you mustn't. There is no need. Really, Rick. We are friends, are we not? We have always been friends. You mustn't try to make it more."

"But, Mary…"

"No. I'm not Enid. I wouldn't do that to you.

Please, Rick. Just leave me be." Her eyes were swimming with tears. She would not cry. She never cried.

One of the Wren cousins came in, thank Heaven above, stopping whatever Rick was going to say next. "Oh, excuse me, I was looking for Mama."

"In the garden, I think," Rick said. Mary took the opportunity to sidle to the door and make her escape, hurrying up the stairs to the safety of her bedroom, where she sat, holding in the tears, listening to the sounds of jollity from the garden, remembering Rick's kiss, and trying not to imagine what might have been.

It seemed like hours before the party slowly wound to a close, but the house was silent when the knock came on her door. It was Aunt Theo, who said, without preamble, "You seem to have successfully chased off your dear lieutenant, Mary. He left very subdued. You have been running from him all week, and what I do not understand, is why you do not let him catch you?"

"He is not my lieutenant. I have not been running. And I do not believe he wishes to catch me."

"I beg to differ, Mary. Young Redepenning is in love with you, or I know nothing about young men. And I have raised six of my own, not to mention all Dr. Wren's students and the strays that find their way here. And you, dear, are in love with him."

Mary picked at her nightgown, not meeting her aunt's eyes. "He... Did he tell you he loves me?"

"He does not need to, Mary. I have eyes in my head. His eyes follow you whenever you are in the room, and he follows after you whenever you leave. When he cannot be with you, he talks about you, and when anyone flirts with you—not that you ever seem to notice—he glares until they slink off."

Mary shook her head. "But, Aunt Theo, he has never said a word."

"Have you let him, Mary, dear?"

She hadn't. She'd seen the look Aunt Theo mentioned and had been afraid to believe it was true. So much so, she had gone out of her way not to be alone with him, had changed the subject whenever he seemed ready to say something serious, and the rare comments she'd been unable to deflect, she had dismissed as Rick the Rogue, flirting as usual. Even tonight, she had refused to let him speak.

But she had to admit he had flirted with no one else. He had been polite and friendly. But he had been attentive only to her. And that kiss...!

Aunt Theo bent over to give her a peck on the cheek. "Think about it, Mary, dear. And pleasant dreams."

Chapter Thirteen

There were no dreams for Mary that night. She lay awake, turning over in her mind all that Rick had said and done since she first met him two and a half months ago in a field in Sussex. In the early hours of the morning, she gave up on sleep and lit her candle to wash and dress, then crept down to the kitchen. Rick would probably leave the inn at first light for his trip to London, but perhaps, just perhaps, she could reach him first.

Rick spent the night awake. Mary's rejection hit

him hard; he'd been so sure that she still cared for him, and not just as a friend. Had he been imagining the sideways looks when she thought he wasn't watching? Were the thousand small services she rendered him, the kindness she always showed him, just signs of affection? Did the blush he could provoke with a compliment mean nothing?

He'd been halfway back to Oxford before the remark about Enid started to bother him, and all the way to his room at the inn before he made sense of it. His foolish Mary thought she had been compromised, and that he had been trapped into proposing. Of course. She had a sense of honor equal to his own, and never a thought of taking advantage of circumstances beyond their control.

He almost turned back then and there, but she had gone to bed. He wouldn't be able to see her until the morning. By everything holy, he was not leaving for London until he got Miss Mary Pritchard on her own and made her listen to him.

In the half-light before dawn, he set out for the Wrens' house, walking his horse carefully on the icy surface of the road. He'd covered perhaps half the distance when he saw her trudging towards him. He knew her immediately, even from several hundred yards in uncertain light.

He dismounted, and waited for her, the anxious uncertainty in his chest easing a little further when her face lit up at the sight of him.

"Running away, Miss Pritchard?"

"Running towards, Lieutenant Redepenning." She blushed then, stopping several paces away, just out of reach. Some perverse imp, still smarting from last night's rejection, kept him silent.

"I brought you a present." She came close enough to hand him a box, tied shut with a ribbon. His heart sank, then. A present. One friend to another. He was reading the signals all wrong, it seemed. He mastered his disappointment enough to smile, to thank her, to hand her the reins, so he could open the box.

It was one of her gingerbread biscuits, cut in the shape of a lady, with an icing dress and bonnet and currant eyes. "A gingerbread lady?"

"A gingerbread bride, Rick," she corrected. "If..." She blushed and stumbled a little over her words, "If... you h-happen to be in n-need of a bride."

"As it happens, I am," he said. Could a man survive such a rebound? From despair to jubilation in a few short words. The birds were beginning their dawn chorus, but none of them sang as loudly as his heart. "I am in need of you, Mary, my love."

Who reached for whom remains forever a mystery, but the box dropped onto the path, unheeded, as their arms wrapped around each other. Their lips met for the second time in their lives, and for many minutes, nothing further was said.

Eventually, Rick found himself considering the logistics of icy roads and wet hedgerows, which recalled him to himself enough to impose discipline on his wayward impulses.

"Mary, I had better put this precious little gingerbread bride safely back in her box before I crush her, and take my own dear runaway bride home to her family. Do you think they will let you come to London with me? If we take Polly, for propriety's sake?"

"To London?"

He put the bride in her box and kissed Mary again. "To stay with my sister while I arrange the wedding. You will marry me straightaway, will you not, Mary? As soon as I can arrange it? So we can spend the rest of my leave together?" He kissed her again, before she could answer.

"Yes, as soon as we can," she affirmed when she was able.

"My dearest love," Rick said.

"Am I your love?"

He loosened his hold enough to lean back so he could see her face. "Surely you know you are."

She shook her head. "I thought I was just the nuisance you had to keep rescuing."

He bent to kiss the tip of her nose. Tall as she was, he was taller.

"Rescuing you is, and has always been, one of my favorite things to do, Mary. I am proud that you have promised me the right to rescue you always."

"Always, Rick, and whenever I run, it will be to you, not from." His beautiful bride giggled. "But right this minute, the gingerbread bride needs rescuing—from the horse!"

Their tender moment ended with Rick chasing the box-chewing horse down the icy lane, while his runaway bride, now truly caught, stood laughing.

THE END

Please consider taking a moment to write a review of *Gingerbread Bride*—even a sentence or two. Honest reviews help other readers to choose books they will enjoy, and help writers to gain visibility in a very cluttered book market.

News and special offers

Subscribe to my newsletter for information about publication dates and more. As a subscriber, you will receive advance information about release dates and special price periods as well as exclusive, subscriber-only special offers. I send a newsletter no more than six times a year.

You will find a subscription link at http://judeknightauthor.com

Acknowledgements

Thank you to my beta readers: my fellow Bluestocking Belles. Your comments and suggestions led to many changes that made the book stronger.

Thank you to Beth Fuge of the Wairarapa Branch of the New Zealand Cake Decorators' Guild, who pulled out all the stops to ice me a bride that did credit to my Mary, so that I could have her on my cover.

As always, a special thank you to my husband, without whose support I would probably forget to eat when I get stuck in the early nineteenth century, and to my sister Sue, who is always my first reader.

Bluestocking Belles

If you love historical romance, then you'll love the Bluestocking Belles.

We're a group of Regency romance authors providing high-quality, entertaining novels of many different styles—and heat levels—for readers who love the Regency world as much as we do.

Our blog, *The Teatime Tattler*, publishes at least twice weekly, with exclusive news, interviews, and scandals set in and around the Regency. We host a monthly book club. The Bluestocking Bookshop is a Facebook Group where writers and readers create impromptu Regency storylines as you watch.

The Belles have committed to publishing at least one box set per year. Proceeds from some of the Belles' joint projects go to the Malala Fund, to support education for young bluestockings around the world.

Find the Bluestocking Belles online:
www.BluestockingBelles.com/
Friend us on Facebook:
www.facebook.com/BellesinBlue
Follow us on Twitter:
@BellesInBlue

The Collected 2015 Editions of the Teatime Tattler

What do the Bluestocking Belles' historical romance characters do when they aren't entertaining readers in our books? Turn to the popular Regency gossip rag, the Teatime Tattler, to find out! In The Collected 2015 Editions of the Teatime Tattler, these bestselling and award-winning HistRom writers bring you a collection of short stories, interviews, cameos, backstories, and scandals, all vignettes connected, one way or another, to the novels and novellas that you know and love, illuminating our characters in ways you cannot find in any of our books.

Malala Fund

The Bluestocking Belles have chosen the Malala Fund as the charity we support, and to which we donate communal royalties. Periodically, we take on projects intended to directly support this cause, which exemplifies our personal values and intentions: the right of girls and women to do whatever they choose with their lives.

For more information about the Malala Fund and the founder, Malala Yousafzai, winner of the 2014 Nobel Peace Prize, go to www.Malala.org

Published books

Candle's Christmas Chair

When Viscount Avery comes to see the best invalid chair maker in the southwest of England he does not expect to find Minerva Bradshaw, the woman who rejected him three years earlier. Or did she? Older and wiser, he wonders if there is more to the story.

For three years, Min Bradshaw has remembered the handsome guardsman who courted her for her fortune. She didn't expect to see him in her workshop, and she certainly doesn't intend to let him fool her again. Even if he is handsomer and more charming than ever.

Farewell to Kindness: Book 1 of *The Golden Redepennings*

Rede believes he has turned his back on compassion and mercy. But he is distracted from the hunt for those who killed his family by his growing attraction for Anne. His feelings for her are a weakness. Or could they instead be a source of strength?

Anne protected her family from scandal and worse by changing their identity. Can she keep Rede from discovering who they are? Can she give him her heart without trusting him? Can she trust him when he has closed himself off to love?

When their enemies link forces, Rede and Anne must face the past in order to claim the future.

A Baron for Becky

Becky is the envy of the courtesans of the demimonde - the indulged mistress of the wealthy and charismatic Marquis of Aldridge. But she dreams of a normal life; one in which her daughter can have a future that does not depend on beauty, sex, and the whims of a man.

Finding herself with child, she hesitates to tell Aldridge. Will he cast her off, send her away, or keep her and condemn another child to this uncertain shadow world?

The devil-may-care face Hugh shows to the world hides a desperate sorrow; a sorrow he tries to drown with drink and riotous living. His years at war haunt him, but even more, he doesn't want to think about the illness that robbed him of the ability to father a son. When he dies, his barony will die with him. His title will fall into abeyance, and his estate will be scooped up by the Crown.

When Aldridge surprises them both with a daring proposition, they do not expect love to be part of the bargain.

Hand-Turned Tales

Dip in, and try my writing for free: four very different tales with a variety of heroes, heroines, villains, and settings.

In *The Raven's Lady*, Felix returns home in disguise after 13 years. He plans to catch a smuggler then take up his viscountcy. He does not expect the smuggler to be Joselyn, his childhood sweetheart. (Short story: 5,500 words)

In *Kidnapped to Freedom*, Phoebe is stolen away from her plantation by a handsome masked pirate. But all is not as it seems. (Short story: 5,100 words)

All that Glisters is set in New Zealand in the 1860s, a time when gold miners poured into the fledgling settlement of Dunedin. Rose is unhappy in the household of her fanatical uncle. Thomas, a young merchant from Canada, offers a glimpse of another possible life. If she is brave enough to reach for it. (Short story: 13,000 words)

The Prisoners of Wyvern Castle is a gothic historical romance set in the world of my novels and novella. Rupert has been imprisoned by his wicked sister, and forced to wed. His new wife, Madeline, has likewise been threatened into saying her vows. Forced into marriage, they find love, but can they find freedom before it is too late? The Prisoners of Wyvern Castle is a prequel to Embracing Prudence, due for publication in 2016. (Novella: 23,500 words)

Coming soon

Prudence in Love: Book 1 of *The Wages of Virtue* and Book 1 of *A Game of Mist and Shadow*

David and Prudence, operatives for one of England's shadowy spymasters, are sent to investigate a spying ring that blackmails aristocrats for access to secrets. Both find friends and family too close to the investigation for comfort.

After what happened last time they worked together, both David and Prue are determined they won't surrender to the strong physical attraction between them. They're professionals. They'll find the blackmailer and the spy behind him, and part again.

But murder, secrets from the past, and love can foil the most determined of plans

A Raging Madness: Book 2 of *The Golden Redepennings*

When Alex Redepenning comes to the funeral of Ella Melville's mother-in-law, he does not expect Ella to turn up in his bedroom, seeking help. They have met twice in the last ten years: once when she married one of Alex's fellow officers under dubious circumstances, and once when she arrived too late to attend her husband's deathbed. They parted rancorously each time.

After what he said at their last meeting Ella had hoped never to see Alex again, but an overheard clandestine conversation leaves her with nowhere else to turn.

Danger follows them; Ella's in-laws want her confined to Bedlam, and someone wants Alex dead. Joining forces is sensible. If they can survive their enemies, the only risk is to their hearts.

Lord Danwood's Dilemma: **Book 1 of** *Danwood's Daughters*

On inheriting from a distant cousin who had no sons, Anthony Simon Wentworth, the new Earl of Danwood, finds his predecessor had a unique way of stacking the odds so that a grandson of his would one day be Earl. Tony has inherited the title and the entailed land, but has no way to support it. To win the non-entailed wealth, he must marry and have a child with one of the former Lord Danwood's eight daughters.

The legitimate daughters live at Danwood Castle in the North York Moors, and in a nearby coastal village, the former Earl had a second family by his wife's sister. The eldest daughter, Sophia, keeps life on an even keel for her two sisters and two brothers, despite a lack of money and the general disapproval of the village.

Tony thinks he will settle the by-blows somewhere out of sight and marry one of the legitimate daughters. But he is distracted by the need to rescue his baseborn relatives from smugglers, the coastguard, an angry farmer or two, the machinations of their aunt—and his growing appreciation of the feisty Sophia.

Connect with Jude Knight

Jude Knight writes strong determined heroines, heroes who can appreciate a clever capable woman, villains you'll love to loathe, and all with a leavening of humour.

After a career in commercial writing, editing, and publishing, Jude Knight returned to her first love, storytelling. *Gingerbread Bride* is a prequel to the novel *Farewell to Kindness*, first of the series: *The Golden Redepennings*.

Follow Jude on Twitter: @JudeKnightBooks
Friend Jude on Facebook:
facebook.com/judeknightbooks
Subscribe to Jude's blog: judeknightauthor.com
Subscribe to Jude's newsletter:
judeknightauthor.com/newsletter/
Follow Jude on Goodreads:
www.goodreads.com/judeknight